P9-BZL-910

ALL ABOARD!

Benedict Blathwayt

HUTCHINSON

ALL ABOARD!
A HUTCHINSON BOOK 978 0 091 79922 9

First edition published in Great Britain by Hutchinson, an imprint of Random House Children's Books
A Random House Group Company

The Runaway Train first published by Julia MacRae, 1995
Little Red Train to the Rescue first published by Julia MacRae, 1997
Faster, Faster, Little Red Train first published by Julia MacRae, 1999
Green Light for the Little Red Train first published by Hutchinson, 2002
The Great Big Little Red Train first published by Hutchinson, 2003
Little Red Train's Race to the Finish first published by Hutchinson, 2006
This edition published as a collection in 2008

1 3 5 7 9 10 8 6 4 2

Hutchinson books are published by Random House Children's Books,
61-63 Uxbridge Road, London W5 5SA

www.**rbooks**.co.uk
www.**kids**at**randomhouse**.co.uk

Addresses for companies within the Random House Group Limited
can be found at: www.randomhouse.co.uk/offices.htm

THE RANDOM HOUSE GROUP Limited Reg. No. 954009

A CIP catalogue for this book is available from the British Library

Printed in Singapore

THE RUNAWAY TRAIN

Duffy Driver overslept.
Everyone was waiting at the
station for the little red train.

When Duffy was ready to start, he saw an old lady running
down the platform. "I'll help you," he said. But he forgot to put
the brake on and the little red train set off down the track . . .
Chuff-chuff, chuff-chuff, whoo . . . oooo

Duffy saw a lorry. "Stop!" Duffy shouted. "I must catch up
with the runaway train!"
"Jump in," cried the lorry driver and off they went after the
little red train . . . *Chuff-chuff, chuff-chuff, whoo . . . oooo . . .*

. . . until they came to a traffic jam.

Duffy saw a boat. "Ahoy there!" Duffy shouted. "I must catch
up with the runaway train!"
"All aboard," cried the boatman and off they all went after the
little red train . . . *Chuff-chuff, chuff-chuff, whoo . . . oooo . . .*

. . . until the river turned away from the railway.

Duffy saw some bicycles. "Help!" Duffy shouted. "I must catch up with the runaway train!"

"Jump on," cried the cyclists and off they all went after the little red train . . . *Chuff-chuff, chuff-chuff, whoo . . . oooo . . .*

. . . until they ran into a flock of sheep.

Duffy saw some ponies. "Whoa!" Duffy shouted. "I must catch up with the runaway train!"
"Up you come," cried the riders and off they all went after the little red train . . . *Chuff-chuff, chuff-chuff, whoo . . . oooo . . .*

. . . until the ponies could go no further.

Duffy saw a tractor. "Halloo!" Duffy shouted. "I must catch up
with the runaway train!"
"Get on then," cried the farmer and off they went after the little
red train . . . *Chuff-chuff, chuff-chuff, whoo . . . oooo . . .*

. . . until they were spotted by a helicopter pilot.

"My last chance!" gasped Duffy. "I must catch up with the runaway train!"

"Climb in quick," said the pilot and Duffy climbed in, while the lorry driver, the boatman, the cyclists, the riders and the farmer all stood and watched . . .

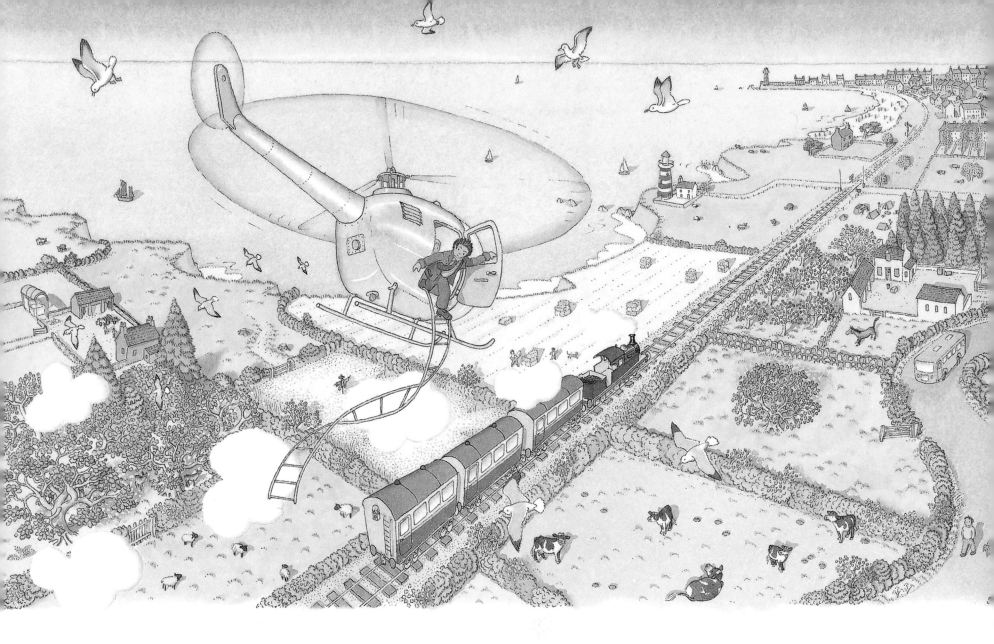

as Duffy caught up with the runaway train . . . *Chuff-chuff,*
chuffitty-chuff, whoo . . . oo . . . oo

And Duffy Driver drove the little red train into the station at
Sandy-on-Sea and spent a lovely lazy afternoon on the beach
before he had to drive back home again.

Chuff-chuff, chuffitty -chuff, whoo . . . eee . . . eee . . .

LITTLE RED TRAIN
TO THE RESCUE

One wet and windy day, Duffy
Driver lit the fire in the little red
train and collected three trucks
from the goods yard.

The trucks were soon loaded and Duffy Driver and the little
red train set off for Birchcombe village, high up in the hills.
Chuff-chuff, chuffitty-chuff...

But as they came round a bend, what did they see...

Animals on the line!
Duffy put on the brakes with a scree...eee...ch
and the little red train stopped just in time.

When the animals were back in the
farmyard, the little red train set off again.
Chuff-chuff, chuffitty-chuff...

But as they came round a bend, what did they see...

The river had flooded the road!
Duffy put on the brakes with a scree...eee...ch
and the little red train stopped just in time.

They rescued the passengers from the bus on
the bridge and the little red train set off again.
Chuff-chuff, chuffitty-chuff...
But as they came round a bend, what did they see...

The wind had blown down a tree!
Duffy put on the brakes with a scree...eee...ch
and the little red train stopped just in time.

Everyone helped to move the tree
and the little red train set off again.
Chuff-chuff, chuffitty-chuff...

But the track got steeper and steeper and
the little red train hotter and hotter until...

P O P! HISSSSS! The safety valve blew off the boiler!
Duffy Driver put on the brakes with a scree...eee...ch
and stopped to let the little red train cool down.

Up in the hills there was snow,
so they set off again more slowly.
Chuff-chuff-chuff, chuu...ff, chuff...itty-chu...ff...
But as they came round a bend, what did they see...

A great pile of snow was blocking the line!
Duffy put on the brakes with a scree...eee...ch
and the little red train stopped just in time.

They all helped to clear the snow
and the little red train set off again.
Chuff-chuff, chuffitty-chuff...

But as they came to the last stretch
of line what did they find...

The points had frozen!
The little red train went off the wrong way.
Duffy put on the brakes with a scree...eee...ch
and the little red train stopped just in time.

The signalman poured hot water on
the points and with a chuff-chuff,
chuffitty-chuff the little red train ran
on towards the station at Birchcombe...

Everyone was there to greet them.
Duffy Driver blew the whistle, whee...eee...eee
and put on the brakes with a scree...eee...ch and the
little red train stopped at the platform just in time.

The passengers climbed down and helped to unload the supplies...

and Duffy Driver was given a special tea by the postmistress.

Then Duffy got back into the driver's cab and after he had blown the whistle, whee...eee...eee, the little red train raced back home. It was downhill all the way.

Chuffitty-chuffitty,
chuffitty-chuff...

FASTER, FASTER, LITTLE RED TRAIN

Duffy Driver was eating his
breakfast when the telephone rang.
"The fast train to Pebblecombe has
broken down," he said. "The Little
Red Train is needed. I'll have to rush."

The passengers from the broken-down train were
cross and worried. "Will the Little Red Train get
there on time, we don't want to miss the fair!"
"All aboard for Pebblecombe," called Duffy Driver.
"We'll go as fast as we can!"
Chuff chuff went the Little Red Train.
Click clack went the wheels on the track.

Their first stop was Newtown.

"Who's for Pebblecombe fair?" shouted Duffy Driver.

"Quick as you can!"

A lady with a big box of strawberries climbed on board.

Whoosh went the steam from the Little Red Train.

Click clack went the wheels on the track.

Click clack clicketty clack.

Next they stopped at Woodhaven.

"Jump on for Pebblecombe fair!" shouted Duffy Driver.

A man with a crate of hens squeezed into the carriage.

"You're running late," he grumbled.

"We're doing our best," Duffy Driver said cheerfully.

Chuff chuff went the Little Red Train.

Click clack went the wheels on the track.

Click clack clicketty clack.

The Little Red Train stopped at Castle Down.
"We're in a hurry," said Duffy Driver, "this train's
for Pebblecombe fair."
A gang of noisy children climbed on board.
Chuff chuff went the Little Red Train.
Chuff chuff, chuffitty chuff...

The next station was Old Harbour.

"Any passengers for Pebblecombe?" called Duffy Driver.

"Is this the right train?" said a boy with a great big dog.

"It is the right train," said Duffy. "And we've no time to lose."

Whoo...eee... whistled the Little Red Train.

Chuff chuff chuffitty chuff.

When they stopped at Hillside station, there were four musicians
waiting on the platform.

"We're playing at Pebblecombe fair," they grumbled,

"and we're going to be late."

"In you get," said Duffy briskly, "we're going as fast as we can."

Whoo…eee… went the Little Red Train. *Whoo…eeee…*

The Little Red Train went faster than ever before.

Click clack went the wheels on the track.

Clicketty clicketty clicketty clack.

"Slow down," said the lady with the strawberries.

"Slow down!" shouted the man with the crate of hens.

"Slow down!" shrieked the boy with the great big dog.

"Steady on!" cried the musicians.

"Faster ... faster!" yelled the noisy children.

But Duffy Driver couldn't hear anyone shouting.
He shovelled more coal into the firebox and
the boiler made more and more steam and
the wheels of the Little Red Train went
faster and faster and faster...
Clicketty clicketty clicketty clicketty clicketty clicketty clack.

And right on time the Little Red Train
pulled into the station at Pebblecombe.

Out got the lady with her box of strawberries, the man with the hens and the boy with the dog and the four musicians and the gang of noisy children.

They thanked Duffy Driver and the Little Red Train for getting them to Pebblecombe so fast. Then they all went off to spend the day at the fair.

Duffy Driver thought he would have another breakfast.
"You're the Little Red Express now," he said as he wiped
down the fenders.

*Whoo...eeee...*went the Little Red Train.

Whoo...oooo...eeee...

GREEN LIGHT FOR THE
LITTLE RED TRAIN

Duffy Driver and the Little Red Train
arrived at the station to pick up their
passengers.

"There's repair work
further up the line,"
said Jack the guard. "You'll
be following a different route
today. Keep going as long as the
lights are green."
"Right," said Duffy.

Sure enough, the points on the railway tracks sent Duffy one way and then another.

The line carried them down into a dark tunnel.

When they came out at the other end, the signal shone green so Duffy and the Little Red Train kept going.

Duffy didn't realize he was in France. Shouldn't I be back on my usual tracks by now? he thought.

When they reached the next station, Duffy slowed down to ask what was going on.

But a noisy electric train clanked up behind them.
PEEP . . . PEEP . . . PEEP, it whistled.
   "Oh, go blow a fuse!" grumbled Duffy, and the
Little Red Train picked up speed again.

Duffy had no idea that he was now in Spain.
But the lights were still green so the Little Red
Train flew along at a tremendous rate.
  Clicketty clicketty clicketty clack

They went so fast and the sun was so hot that the Little Red Train's water tanks ran dry and the needle on the pressure gauge pointed to DANGER.

"Water!" shouted Duffy, putting on the brake. "We need water or the train will explode!"

Luckily there was water just ahead.
Everyone jumped down and helped
to fill the Little Red Train's water tanks.
TOOT . . . TOOT . . . TOOT, tooted
an impatient freight train behind them.
"Oh, nuts and bolts to you!" hissed Duffy.
But the signal far down the line shone
green so off they had to go again.

The Little Red Train's coal bunker was almost empty.
Duffy stopped to find out where he could buy some
more coal. But nobody understood what he was saying.

Duffy didn't know it, but he was in Italy.

BARP . . . BARP . . . BARP, hooted a
cross diesel train behind them.

"Oh, go pop your rivets!" shouted Duffy.

But the signal lights glowed green so Duffy blew the whistle and let off the brake and they were soon speeding along again at a sizzling pace.

Whoo . . . ooo . . . eee

Chuffitty chuffitty chuffitty chuff

When the last lump of coal was gone,
the fire in the firebox went out and the
Little Red Train stopped.

"We're stuck!" cried Duffy.

So everyone jumped down and
gathered dry wood until the Little Red
Train's coal bunker was full.

But . . .

. . . *HOO . . . HOO . . . HOO*, honked a furious express train behind them.

"Oh, smoke and smuts to you!" yelled Duffy.

He lit a new fire in the firebox and soon the Little Red Train had built up enough steam to get going again.

This is the longest detour I've ever had to take, thought Duffy. But he had no idea just how far north he had come. He opened the throttle as wide as it would go and the Little Red Train's wheels spun and the wind whistled past until . . .

. . . a signal ahead shone RED!

Duffy heaved on the brake and the wheels locked and the
Little Red Train slid along in a shower of sparks and stopped
just an inch away from the end of the line.

Duffy was so tired that he didn't realize he was on a ferry. He knew he had done his best and obeyed signals when they were green and stopped when they were red – so he settled down in his cab for a well-earned snooze.

Duffy woke with a jolt when the ferry docked. He
was told by a rather cross man to get going.

The Little Red Train sped through the night and
the signals shone green all the way.

"Where have you been?" asked Jack the guard when they arrived back at the station.

Duffy shrugged his shoulders. "Your guess is as good as mine," he said, "but it's really good to be home."

The Little Red Train let out a great sigh of steam.

Whoo . . . eee . . . whoo . . . eee . . . eee . . .

THE GREAT BIG
LITTLE RED TRAIN

Duffy and Jack were sitting in Jack's guard's van having a quiet cup of tea when a large lorry drove past the railway sidings.

"Haven't you got any work to do, mate?" the lorry driver yelled at Duffy. "I'm not surprised. A train that old and small is no use to anyone! It belongs in a museum; or on the scrap heap."

Surely the Little Red Train doesn't look that old and useless, thought Duffy.

Just then Duffy and Jack had three unexpected visitors.

"The furniture for my autumn sale is stuck at the docks," said the showroom manager.

"I want gravel from the quarry for my concrete mixers," grumbled the cement works foreman.

"I need to collect timber from the forest," said the sawmill owner.

"Why aren't the lorries delivering by road as usual?" Duffy asked his visitors.

"Terrible traffic," they groaned, "roadworks, breakdowns, faulty traffic lights. We were wondering if the Little Red Train could help us. The old track and trucks are still there somewhere."

"We'll see what we can do,"
said Duffy.
"Don't forget the oil can, Jack!"

The Little Red Train set off at top speed.
Clicketty clack, clicketty clack
Clicketty clicketty clicketty clack

SLOW

"I can see why the lorries aren't getting anywhere,"
Duffy called out to Jack in the guard's van.

When the Little Red Train reached the docks, Duffy and Jack
kept a look out for the old railway sidings.

"Here they are!" yelled Jack, jumping down to oil the points.
"And there are plenty of old trucks too."

Duffy hitched up the trucks to the Little Red Train with
Jack's van at the back.

The old railway line led right along
the dockside and under a huge crane.

The crane lifted the containers of furniture out of the ship's hold and lowered them onto the trucks.

When all the trucks were loaded,
the Little Red Train steamed out of the
old sidings and back onto the main line.
   "Off to the quarry now," said Duffy.
   Huff-chuff . . . huff-chuff . . . huff-chuff went
the steam from the Little Red Train's pistons.
   Creak . . . squeak went the rusty wheels on
the trucks. *Cree . . . eak, squee . . . eeak*

When they arrived at the quarry the old railway line
was almost completely hidden under a layer of dust.
   "There are a lot of old gravel trucks here," said Jack.
"Let's hitch them up at the front."

One by one the quarry hopper
filled the trucks with gravel.

"Off to the forest now," said Duffy. "I hope the Little Red Train is strong enough to pull all these trucks."

Huffitty-chuffitty . . . huffitty-chuffitty . . . huffitty-chuffitty puff went the smoke from the Little Red Train's funnel.

Creak . . . screech went the truck wheels on the rusty track. *Cree . . . ee . . . eak, scree . . . ee . . . eech*

When they arrived at the forest, Duffy and Jack soon found the overgrown tracks and some flatbed trucks hidden in the brambles. Duffy guided the Little Red Train onto the old tracks and hooked up the trucks at the front.

The foresters loaded lots of long logs onto
the trucks and they were ready to go.
"Let's head for home!" said Duffy.

The Little Red Train's wheels spun, and smoke and steam puffed furiously from its funnel.

Huffitty-puffitty . . . huffitty-puffitty . . . huffitty-puffitty puff

Very, very slowly the long chain of trucks – with the tree trunks from the forest, the gravel from the quarry and the furniture from the docks – followed the Little Red Train out onto the main line.

And right at the back of the very, very long train came Jack's guard's van.

Whoo . . . ooo . . . eee whistled the great big Little Red Train.

Duffy waved to the lorry drivers who were still stuck in a traffic jam.

When Duffy and Jack arrived home the showroom manager and the cement works boss and the sawmill owner were ready to help them unload. "Thank goodness for the Little Red Train," they said. "We'd have been stuck without you!"

Duffy and Jack cleaned and oiled the trucks.
And then they gave the Little Red Train a
shiny new coat of paint.

"We're ready for our next job now," said
Duffy proudly. "Well done, Little Red Train."

LITTLE RED TRAIN'S
RACE TO THE FINISH

Duffy Driver and Jack the guard were fed up.

"Those Swish Trains," said Jack. "They're taking over! And now they want the route to Barnacle Bay."

"The Little Red Train will have nothing to do!" said Duffy.

The Swish Train drivers just laughed at Duffy and Jack.

"Your train is old and slow," they said.

"Everybody loves the Little Red Train," said Duffy. "It's not *that* slow!"

"Prove it then!" sneered the drivers. "We'll race you to Barnacle Bay.
Whoever wins the race, wins the route."

Duffy and Jack got ready for the big race.

"We've got to win by miles," whispered the Swish driver,

"so no one will want to use the Little Red Train ever again."

Down went the flag . . .
They were off!
Puff chuff, puff chuff
went the Little Red Train.

Sweeeeeeeeesh! went the Swish Train as it sped past and out of sight.
"Oh, rust and dust!" said Duffy.

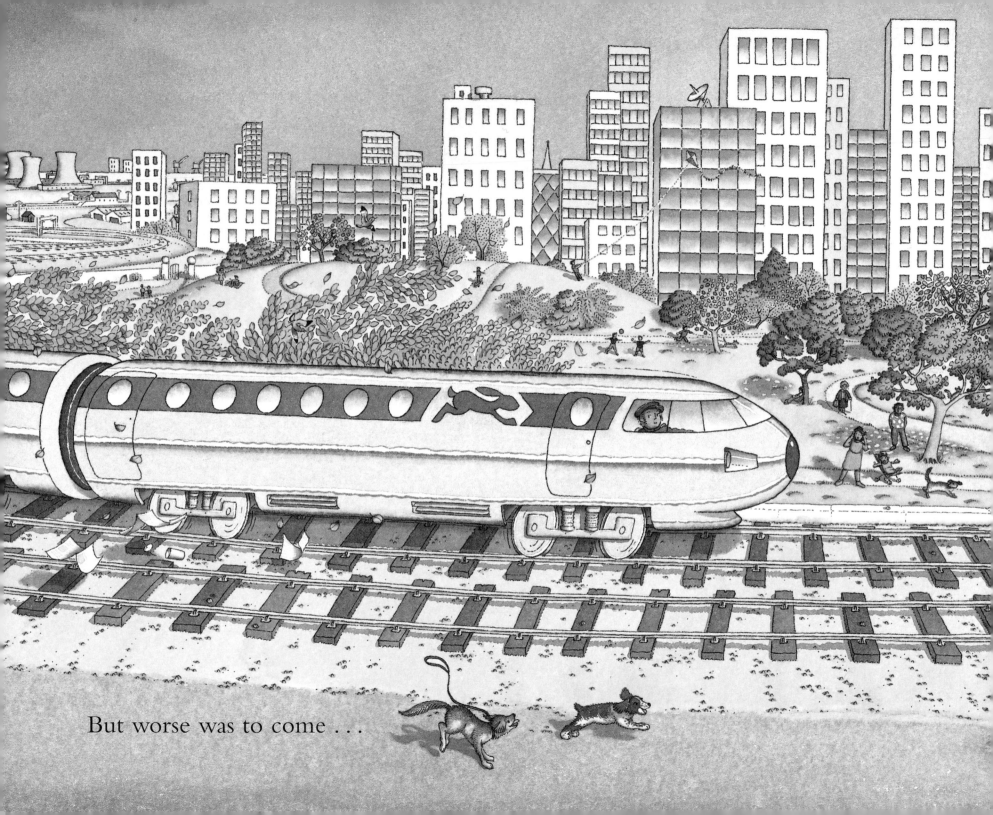

But worse was to come . . .

At the very first hill, the Little Red
Train's wheels began to spin.
   "There's oil on the tracks," said Duffy.
"I wonder how it got there."

The passengers pushed the Little Red Train over the top of the hill.

"We can still catch up!"
yelled Jack.
But worse was to come . . .

Sheep on the line!

Duffy put on the brakes with a *screeeeech* and they stopped just in time.

"I wonder who left the gate open," said Duffy.

At the next station the Swish Train driver had stopped
for a cup of tea. He seemed very surprised indeed to
see the Little Red Train.

Duffy steamed past without slowing down.

Chuff chuff chuffitty chuff

But soon enough the Swish Train passed them again and
disappeared into the distance with a great *swoooooooosh!*
"Oh, coke and clinker!" said Duffy.
But worse was to come . . .

Suddenly the Little Red Train went off in the wrong direction.

"Someone's switched the points," said Duffy. "But who?"

Duffy put on the brakes and started to go back.

"Whoa!" said Jack. "Keep going! This is the *old* way to Barnacle Bay. It will lead back on to the main line and straight to the finish."

So the Little Red Train kept going.
"Hold on tight!" shouted Duffy.

"There hasn't been a train along here for years," said Duffy.
"Don't slow down!" Jack shouted from his van.

When they reached the main line again,
Jack switched the points. Now the Little
Red Train was back on the right track.

"There's Barnacle Bay!"
cried Duffy.
  "And here comes the
Swish Train!" yelled Jack.

The roar of the Swish Train grew louder and louder.
The Little Red Train went faster and faster . . .
Clicketty clack, clicketty clack, clicketty clicketty clicketty clack!

But the Swish Train could not catch up and the Little Red
Train won the race!

"Hooray!" shouted the passengers.

"Hooray!" shouted Duffy and Jack.

Whoooooosssssssh went the steam from the Little Red Train.

When the celebrations were over, Duffy,
Jack and the Little Red Train headed home.
  "I think Barnacle Bay is my favourite
place in the world," said Jack.
  "Me too," said Duffy. And he blew the
Little Red Train's whistle, long and loud.
  Whooooo . . . oooooooooo . . . eeeeeeeeeeeeeee!